Box-Head Boy

To my family and friends

Cover design and page layout by Circus Design

Library of Congress Cataloging-in-Publication Data

Winn, Christine M.
        Box-head boy / by Christine M. Winn, with David Walsh; illustrated by Christine M. Winn.
                p.   cm.
        Summary: Denny spends so much time watching TV that one day his head ends up inside the set.
        ISBN 0-925190-88-8 (acid-free)
        [1. Television—Fiction.   2. Imagination—Fiction.]   I. Walsh, David. II. Title.
PZ7.W72974Bo 1996
[Fic]—dc20   95-43560
                                                               CIP
                                                               AC

First Printing: March 1996
Printed in the United States of America

00 99 98 97 96   7 6 5 4 3 2 1

Published by Fairview Press, 2450 Riverside Avenue South, Minneapolis, MN 55454.

For a current catalog of Fairview Press titles, please call this Toll-Free number: 1-800-544-8207

Publisher's Note: Fairview Press publishes books and other materials related to the subjects of physical health, mental health, chemical dependency, and other family issues. Its publications, including *Box-Head Boy,* do not necessarily reflect the philosophy of Fairview Hospital and Healthcare Services or their treatment programs.

The paper used in this publication meets the minimum requirements of American National Standard for Information Sciences—Permanence of Paper for Printed Library Materials, ANSI Z329.48-1984.

Box-Head Boy

by

Christine **M**. **W**inn

with **D**avid **W**alsh, Ph.D.

Illustrated by

Christine **M**. **W**inn

Fairview Press

Fairview Press
Minneapolis, Minnesota

Denny was like any other kid.
He hated lima beans and loved chocolate. He played basketball with his friends. He made cardboard fins for himself and his dog Pesky, and they pretended to be sharks to scare the neighbors. Denny won second place at the science fair. And he was famous for squirting milk through his nose during lunch at school.

But more than anything else, Denny watched TV, or "the box" as his parents called it. Denny turned on the TV whenever he was in the house. He watched cartoons as he ate his breakfast. After school he watched a show about monkey soldiers who protected the earth from nasty alien creatures. He surfed the channels when he did his homework. Before bed, he watched cop shows and monster movies.

Now and then Denny's mom chased him outside. "Go play, Dennis! You're spending too much time looking at that silly box," she complained. "If you keep watching that garbage, you'll turn into a TV."

Denny just let his mom cool off, then snuck back in time to catch the monster movie matinee.

One day after school, as always,
Denny was watching his favorite programs on TV.

"Hey, Denny! Yo, Denny!" his friends shouted from the yard.
"Come out and play!"

But Denny didn't answer them. He just kept watching TV.

The more TV Denny watched, the closer he moved toward the box. He moved so close his nose touched the screen.

Denny turned off the real world and focused only on the box. He stopped caring about anyone or anything except the box.

Then, in a blink of an eye, Denny's head went inside the TV. Before he knew it, he had changed from a regular boy into a box-head boy.

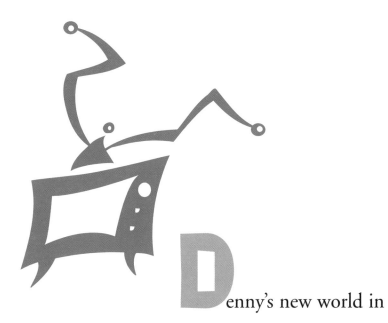

Denny's new world in the box was like a dream come true. "Cool!" thought Denny. "This is great! I can see monkey soldiers all around my head. It's like I'm hanging out with them!"

Denny wondered about

his favorite cop show, and instantly the characters appeared in front

of him. "Wow! I can put on any show I want, just by thinking about

it," Denny realized. "I can even watch stuff my parents won't let me."

Denny used his mind to put on lots of shows all at once.

He filled the box with superheroes, monsters, cops, bad guys, war

movies, cooking shows, and talk shows. "Neat!" he thought.

The images danced and laughed around Denny's head. "Hey, fun!" thought Denny. "I wonder if they'll let me play?" But when he opened his mouth, Denny found he had no voice. When he tried to tap someone on the shoulder, he discovered he couldn't move his arms. "This stinks!" Denny thought, while he listened and watched the images do everything he couldn't. "I can't talk, I can't touch anything," he thought, "and there's all this great food in here, but I can't taste it or even smell it. This isn't fair, it's not fair at all."

Suddenly, out of the dark, a lizard monster leaped toward Denny's face. It frightened him, and all the images around him started acting wild. The characters Denny had always loved seemed scary now. They fought and screamed and shot weapons right under his nose.

"This is a nightmare!" thought Denny. "I want to go home. I want my mom and dad, and Pesky, and my friends. I miss my real life!"

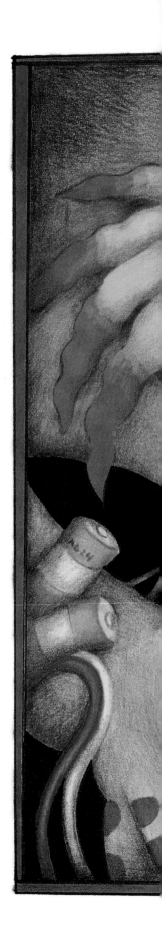

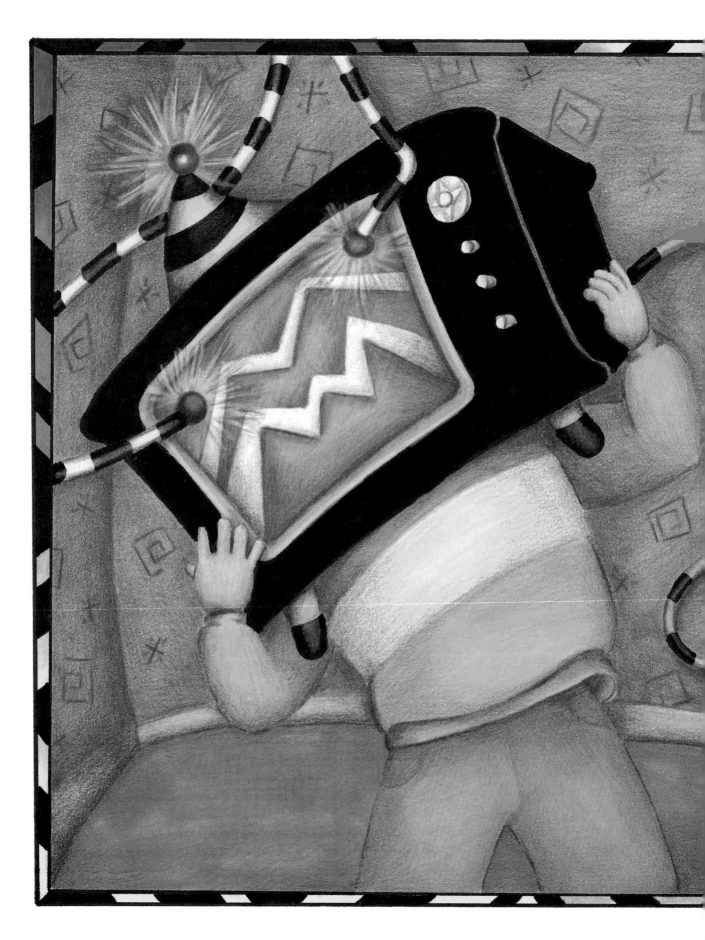

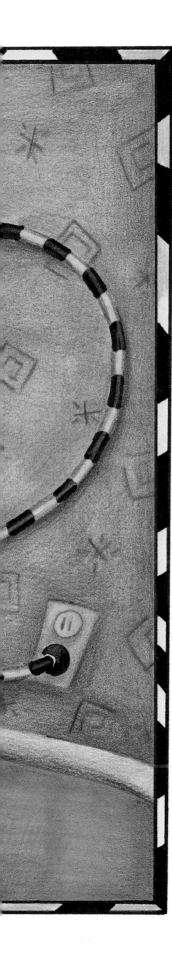

"**I**'m getting out of here," Denny decided. First he tried to shake the box off his shoulders. Then he went from channel to channel looking for his home. Then he tried to shut the TV off. "Nothing's working," he worried. "I'm still in this stupid box."

Just when he was about to give up, Denny turned to a channel with nothing but static. "Maybe these fuzzy lines will help me out," he hoped. Instantly all the characters disappeared. "All right! Here I go!" thought Denny excitedly.

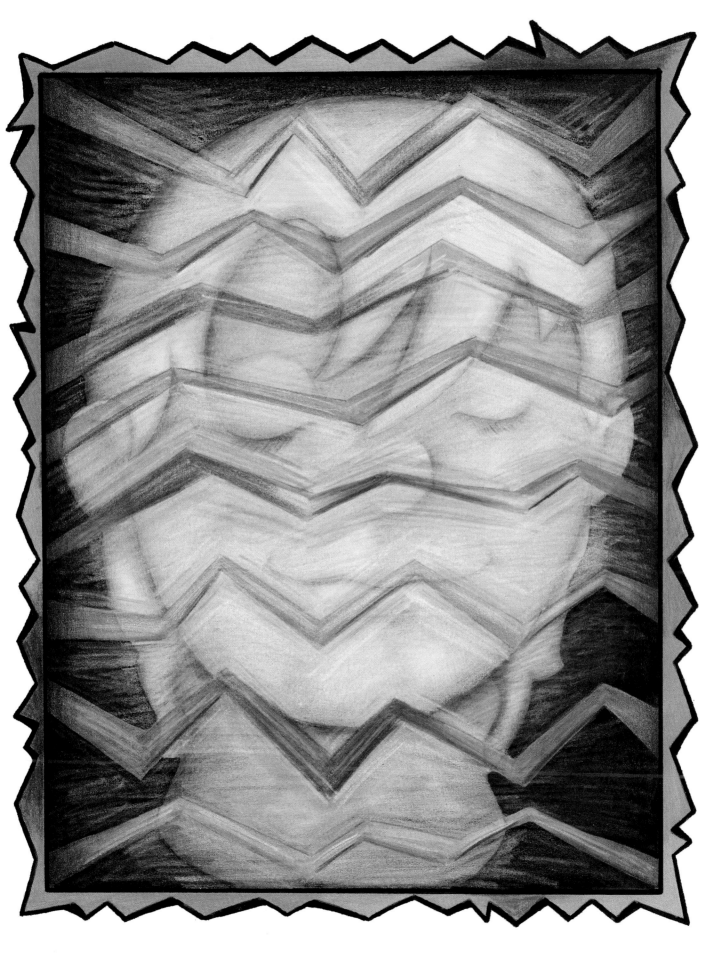

When Denny was alone with only the static, he began thinking about all the fun things he used to do. He imagined himself playing with his friends and his dog. He thought about eating a big piece of chocolate cake and building mountains out of his mashed potatoes. He remembered how great it was to lie in the grass and feel the sun on his face. Denny closed his eyes and let his mind take him home.

When Denny opened

his eyes again, he was out of the box. Quickly he reached over and

turned the TV off.

"That big ugly lizard can't get me out here!" he said,

smiling at the sound of his own voice. Then he felt Pesky's wet nose

sniffing his hand.

"Pesky!" Denny laughed as he petted his dog. "Wow! Is it great

to see you!"

Denny heard his mom shout from the kitchen, "Dennis, you

have five minutes to wash for supper!" Denny could smell meatloaf

and fresh rolls cooking. "And no eating supper in front of the box

tonight," ordered his mom.

"That's fine with me, Mom," Denny agreed willingly.

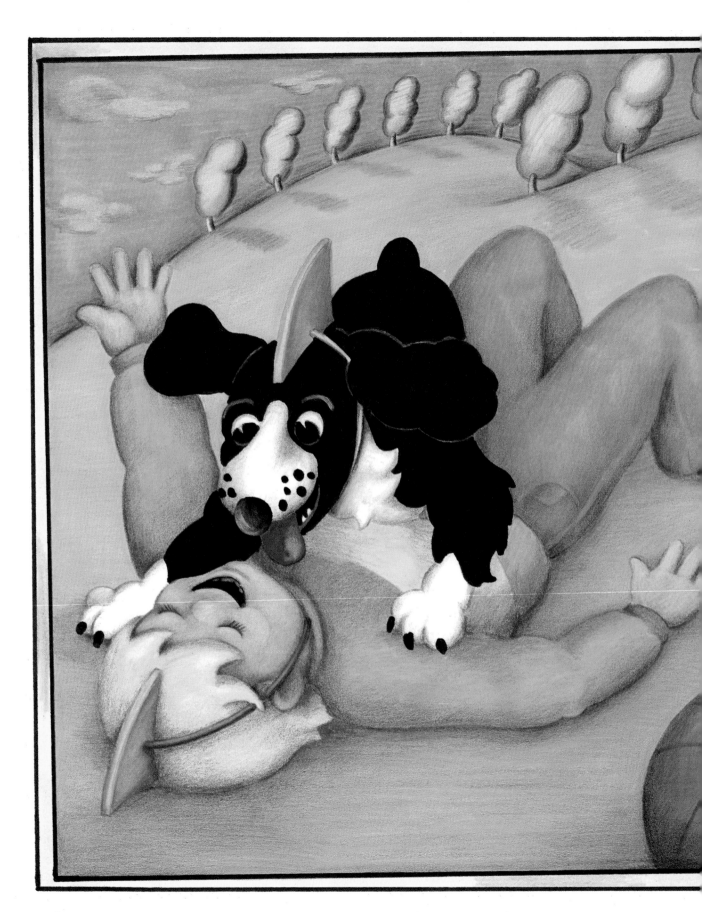

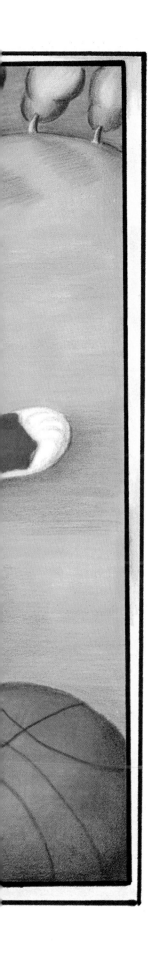

After supper, Denny and Pesky put on their fins and swam with the dolphins in the backyard. Later he played basketball with friends. And before bed, Denny started reading *The Adventures of Tom Sawyer*, a book his parents had given him months ago.

From that day on Denny watched only a little TV. Instead, he spent most of his time doing real stuff in the real world.

Other children's books by Fairview Press:

Alligator in the Basement, by Bob Keeshan, TV's Captain Kangaroo
illustrated by Kyle Corkum

Clover's Secret, by Christine M. Winn with David Walsh, Ph.D.
illustrated by Christine M. Winn

Monster Boy, by Christine M. Winn with David Walsh, Ph.D.
illustrated by Christine M. Winn

My Dad Has HIV, by Earl Alexander, Sheila Rudin, Pam Sejkora
illustrated by Ronnie Walter Shipman

DATE DUE

DEC 1 9 2001	

GAYLORD   PRINTED IN U.S.A.